THE MEANWHILE
ADVENTURES

RODDY DOYLE

Have you read
Roddy Doyle's
other fantastic
children's books?

THE GIGGLER
TREATMENT

ROVER SAVES
CHRISTMAS

THE MEANWHILE ADVENTURES

RODDY DOYLE

Illustrated by Brian Ajhar

■SCHOLASTIC

Scholastic Children's Books,
Euston House, 24 Eversholt Street,
London NW1 1DB, UK
a division of Scholastic Ltd
London ~ New York ~ Toronto ~ Sydney ~ Auckland
Mexico City ~ New Delhi ~ Hong Kong

First published by Scholastic Ltd, 2004
This edition published by Scholastic Ltd, 2005

10 digit ISBN 0 439 96331 1
13 digit ISBN 978 0439 96331 2

Printed and bound by Nørhaven Paperback A/S, Denmark

5 7 9 10 8 6 4

To Rene'e
R. D.

To Kevin, Jake and Eric
B. A.

CHAPTER ONE

Once upon a time there was a little girl who lived in a house made of gingerbread—

Boring.

There was once a little girl called Kayla Mack, and she lived in a house made of—

Still boring. Start again.

OK.

A little girl called Kayla Mack lived in a—

Still boring. Start again. And this is your last chance.

OK. One, two, three –

Kayla Mack stood on the cat's head. She pressed her foot on the head until it squeaked. She pressed three times and ran out the back door of her house. By the way, the house wasn't made of gingerbread. And, by the way, the cat squeaked because it was plastic. The squeak was a signal to her friend, Victoria.

How's that, so far?

Not bad, so far. Continue.

On her way out the door she met her father, Mister Mack. He was carrying a machine gun.

"Who are you?" said Kayla.

"It's not a machine gun," said Mister Mack. "It's a saw. I just invented it."

"Who are you?"

"I know it looks like a machine

gun," said Mister Mack. "But it's a saw. Look. I'll show you how it works."

But Kayla wasn't interested. Once you've seen one machine gun, you've seen them all. She kept running.

CHAPTER TWO

Mister Mack was happy.

But Kayla wasn't.

Because she was stuck in a hedge.

"Who are you!"

The hedge was a big hairy one, between the Macks' garden and her friend Victoria's garden. There was a hole in the hedge and it was a good shortcut, if you could find the hole. And that was the problem. Kayla had missed the hole. She was right beside it, but up to her knees in leaves and little branches that grabbed at clothes and wouldn't let go.

"Who are you!"

Two lizards lived in the hedge, and some budgies who'd escaped from the pet shop – they pretended they were sparrows – and a rat that only ate fresh vegetables.

Boring.

He used to eat everything. In his life, so far, he had eaten thirty-six dead animals, and three live ones. He'd eaten 365 different types of biscuits. He'd eaten car tyres, crisps and half a pedestrian bridge.

But not any more.

"I never liked being a rat," he was telling Kayla, although she wasn't listening.

She was shouting for Victoria to come and rescue her.

"Who are youuuuuu!"

CHAPTER THREE

Mister Mack was happy. And that was nice, because it was a long time since Mister Mack had been happy. Seventy-three days, exactly. If you counted back seventy-three days – and Mister Mack did it all the time – you came to the day when Mister Mack lost his job in the biscuit factory.

"Nobody's eating biscuits any more," said his boss, Mister Kimberley. "They're all too healthy."

They were standing beside Mister Mack's desk. There was a set of weighing scales on the desk, a photograph of his family and a big bronze fig-roll:

ALL-IRELAND BISCUIT-TESTING CHAMPION – 2004.

"Nobody's eating biscuits any more," said Mister Kimberley. "Even the rats have stopped eating biscuits."

Mister Mack was a biscuit tester. The factory made 365 different types of biscuits, a biscuit for every day of the year. And Mister Mack tested them all. He measured and weighed them. He crumbled and smelled them. And he tasted them. That was his favourite part of the job. He bit with his teeth, but his tongue did most of the work. And Mister Mack's tongue was the best in the biscuit business. He could tell if a biscuit had gone even ten minutes past its best-before date. He could tell if the jam in the middle wasn't jammy enough, if the chocolate on the outside wasn't milky enough. Mister Mack was the best biscuit tester in Ireland.

"I'm sorry," said Mister Kimberley. "But we have to stop making the biscuits."

"All of them?" said Mister Mack.

"No," said Mister Kimberley. "We're keeping the cream crackers."

"Oh no!" said Mister Mack.

"One a day," said Mister Kimberley, "we're going to stop making the biscuits. Until we're left with just the good old cream crackers."

"We're healthy and nutritious, and sneaky and malicious," said the cream cracker in Mister Mack's head, the one that always spoiled his daydreams. "Isn't that interesting?"

Mister Mack hated the cream crackers.

"Does that mean I'm fired?" he asked Mister Kimberley.

"No, no," said Mister Kimberley. "Don't worry. We want you to test the cream crackers."

"No way!" said Mister Mack.

He picked up his bronze fig-roll and walked out of the factory and all the way home, because he couldn't remember where he'd parked his car. In fact, he was so upset, he couldn't remember if he owned a car. (Interesting fact: he didn't.)

But Mister Mack wasn't the kind of man who stayed upset for long. By the time he got home – it took him four hours – he'd decided that, if he couldn't be a biscuit tester, then he'd be something else instead.

He walked in the back door. His wife, Billie Jean Fleetwood-Mack, was standing on the kitchen table. She'd just jumped there, from the top of the fridge.

"I'm going to become an inventor," said Mister Mack.

"What kind of inventor?" asked Billie Jean.

"A mad one," said Mister Mack.

CHAPTER FOUR

All that had happened seventy-three days before. Meanwhile, Kayla was still stuck in the hedge.

"Have you any idea how many calories there are in a fig-roll?" asked the rat.

Kayla yelled.

"Who are you!"

Where was her friend, Victoria? What was keeping her?

"It's shocking," said the rat. "All those calories, going straight to my hips. And there was me in that factory eating away, for years."

"Tweet tweet," said a budgie. "Will you listen to that eejit."

"Tweet tweet," said his chum. "I'm going back to the pet shop."

"Last one back is a chicken nugget, tweet tweet."

"Chicken nuggets?" said the rat. "Those things should be banned. The chickens of the world should be ashamed of themselves."

"Who are you!"

Kayla was four years old and she could say a lot more than "Who are you?" but, because everyone she knew loved her so much, they understood exactly what she meant, so she usually didn't bother saying anything else. But she could when she wanted to.

Here is an example of something that Kayla could say:

"If you don't shut up, I'll break your head."

She said it now to the rat.

"Charming," said the rat.

"Who are you!!"

Where was Victoria?

CHAPTER FIVE

Meanwhile, Mister Mack walked into the sitting room. His two sons, Robbie and Jimmy Mack, were in there. They were on the floor, playing a game called War.

Rules: War is a game for two or more players. Players shout "War!" at each other until they become bored or hungry or are bursting for a wee, and leave the room. The last player in the room is the winner. Also, the game ends if someone else walks into the room. There is no time limit.

(Interesting fact: The longest game of War has been going on for more than twenty-eight years, in Tipperary. The two remaining players, the O'Hara twins, Eddie and Kenny, are now thirty-nine. They haven't slept since 1976.)

Anyway, Mister Mack rushed into the room. (And the War ended.)

"Look, lads," he said.

"Nice machine gun, Dad," said Jimmy.

"It's not a machine gun," said Mister Mack. "It's a saw. Look."

He put a piece of wood against the wall. He stood back and pointed his saw at the wood.

"Now, lads. Watch."

The air was suddenly full of wood chips, and noise.

The noise stopped. Mister Mack looked pleased.

"See?"

He pointed at the wood, which was

now two pieces of wood.

"I sawed it."

"Fair enough, Dad," said Robbie. "But you smashed the windows as well."

"And the door and the sofa and the picture of Granny," said Jimmy.

"Oh," said Mister Mack.

He looked around the room. Some of the padding from the sofa had landed on his head.

"Ah, well," he said.

He looked at the wood again.

"It just needs fine tuning."

He patted the saw, and smiled. At last, he had invented something that would make him some money. He had been an inventor for only seventy-three days but, already, Mister Mack had invented lots of things. Mousetraps that tickled the mice until they promised to leave the house. A special brush for getting fluff off duvet covers—

Boring.

A bomb that made big men poo. A fridge that said "Go to the shops" when you opened the door and it was empty. Little batteries to put into bigger dead batteries. A machine that turned green recycling bins into plastic bags. And the toilet was really special: you could wee and wash your hands at the same time. These were all Mister Mack's inventions. The house was full of them, and they were all great.

But nobody wanted them. And Mister Mack was running out of money. The fridge said "Go to the shops!" before he even touched the handle.

The saw was Mister Mack's last chance.

He knew it would work. He just needed a little more time to make it perfect, and a little more money to keep them going.

He smiled again at Jimmy and Robbie.

"I'm off to the bank," said Mister Mack.

"Oh oh," said Robbie.

"Do you want to come with me?" asked Mister Mack.

"Are you sure about this, Dad?" said Jimmy.

"Yes," said Mister Mack. "We'll be back in plenty of time for dinner."

"But," said Robbie.

"But," said Jimmy.

"But," said Mister Mack, "the bank will be closed if we don't hurry up. Come on, boys."

Mister Mack went out the front door, and Jimmy and Robbie ran after him.

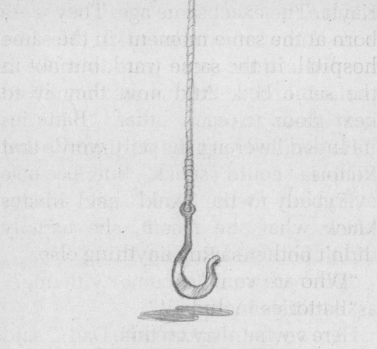

CHAPTER SIX

Meanwhile, Victoria rescued Kayla.

How?

Good question. She did it with another of Mister Mack's inventions. A hook for pulling children out of hedges.

"Who are you?"

"Batteries included!"

Victoria was four, the same age as Kayla. The exact same age. They were born at the same moment, in the same hospital, in the same ward, but not in the same bed. And now they lived next door to each other. "Batteries included" weren't the only words that Victoria could speak, but because everybody who loved her always knew what she meant, she usually didn't bother saying anything else.

"Who are you?"

"Batteries included!"

Here's what they meant:

KAYLA: What kept you?

VICTORIA: Well, I couldn't hear you because my mammy was singing and then she stopped and I heard you but I was a bit hungry so I made a ham and banana and bread sandwich, and then I had to put my jigsaw back in the box and then I couldn't find my boots and I found them in the fridge and here I am and stop complaining and grab the hook.

Kayla leaned out and took the hook. She put it under the belt of her trousers. A rope went from the hook to the back of Victoria's bike. Victoria was on the bike, on top of her slide. She put her foot on the pedal and pushed. She cycled down the slide and Kayla flew out of the hedge. She landed behind Victoria, and Victoria kept pedalling. And she was doing fifty miles an hour, right through a flock of lost budgies.

"Holy Mother of God, what was that – tweet tweet?"

And she was going even faster when they got to the front gate.

"Who are you!"

"Batteries included!"

The speed limit is thirty miles an hour, on the road, but the bike was doing sixty, on the path. Victoria turned right before they reached the road, and the bike headed straight towards a lady and her daughters. There were three daughters, and they were all the same age.

"Oh, good gracious!" said the lady.

"Oh, good gracious!" said the first triplet.

"Oh, good gracious!" said the second triplet.

"Oh, stop copying *her* all the time!" said the third one.

The lady and two of the triplets jumped out of the way, on to the road, which was safer because the trucks and cars were only doing thirty. The third triplet jumped on to the garden wall, which was even safer because the wall was doing nothing.

Kayla and Victoria went in one direction, so they didn't see Mister Mack or Robbie or Jimmy, because they were going in the other direction.

Jimmy and Robbie heard the triplets.

"Did you see that?"

"Did you see that?"

"I'm much more interested in *this*!"

But they didn't look back to see the triplets or to see what this was.

(Interesting fact: *this* was a slug, and it was wearing a crash helmet, and it was charging very slowly across the path.) They'd seen the triplets three times already that day. They had to run to keep up with Mister Mack. He was very excited. He took the saw off his shoulder and swung it in the air.

"Hello, Missis O'Janey," he called to one of his neighbours.

Missis O'Janey was in her garden. She was bending down, looking at a slug with a crash helmet. She looked up, with a smile ready for Mister Mack – and she saw the saw. She screamed and ran back into her house.

But Mister Mack didn't notice. He was now looking at all the other people who were screaming and running away. The street was full of them. People screaming, slugs with crash helmets.

"Interesting," said Mister Mack.

He walked on one of the slugs.

No, he didn't.

He carefully stepped over it and—

Boring.

His foot landed on two others and, if it hadn't been for their crash helmets, they'd have been squashed.

"It just goes to show you," said a slug. "You should never go out without your crash helmet."

"Yes," said his friend. "But I still wish mine was red."

Mister Mack walked on.

The bank was straight ahead. He could see the big sign – BRING ALL YOUR MONEY OVER HERE – on the roof. The bank was right beside the building that used to be the pet shop, Cuddly Pets. Cuddly Pets had closed down the day before because of the budgie shortage, and it was now a butcher shop, Tasty Meat.

Mister Mack passed a flock of budgies. They were on the path, outside Tasty Meat.

"Where's the pet shop, tweet tweet?" asked a budgie.

"I don't know," said another budgie. "And I'm not going in there to find out, tweet tweet."

But Mister Mack didn't notice the budgies.

He was at the door of the bank when Jimmy and Robbie caught up with him. They wanted to save their father, because they loved him—

Boring.

But what they didn't realize was, they had just saved the world.

How?

I thought you were bored.

Tell me.

OK.

CHAPTER SEVEN
HOW JIMMY AND ROBBIE MACK
SAVED THE WORLD

They nearly stood on a slug.

CHAPTER EIGHT

Mister Mack pushed the door of the bank and—

Hey!

Yes?

What about Robbie and Jimmy saving the world and all that?

OK. Here goes –

THE SLUGS OF DUBLIN

The slugs of Dublin had decided to take over the world. They arranged a meeting in a hotel, but it took some of them so long to get there that the hotel had been knocked down and was a car park by the time they arrived. So, they had their meeting in the car park.

"Hands up who wants to take over the world?" said the leader.

"We don't have hands," said a slug.

"What's the world?" said another.

"The world's a big, round place," said the leader. "And just raise your feelers instead."

The leader counted the feelers.

"That looks like everybody in favour," he said.

"No," said a slug. "Mine isn't up. It just looks like it is."

"OK," said the leader. "All except one are in favour of taking over the world."

The slugs cheered.

"Right," said the leader. "Let's get out there and kick some human posterior. But first, everybody has to wear crash helmets. There are millions of feet and tyres out there."

"I want a red one!" shouted a slug.

"There's only one red one," said the leader, "and I'm having it."

"Not fair!" said the slug.

"Are we ready?" said the leader.

"Yessss!" thousands of slugs shouted.

"Charge!"

And, twenty-seven days later, the slugs were still charging.

"No legs good, two legs bad! No legs good, two legs bad!"

And they were charging across the path when Mister Mack stood on two of them. And then, as they watched Mister Mack's feet move away, Jimmy

and Robbie very nearly stood on them.

"No legs good – God!"

Jimmy's lace whacked a crash helmet. The sole of his trainer looked like a slowly moving cliff beside them, right against them. They watched it lift and slowly fall back toward them.

"Ah here," said a slug. "I'm going home."

"Me too," said his pal.

The other slugs watched their friends turning back, and most of them followed.

"Come back!" yelled the leader.

"Not unless you give me the red one," said a slug.

"No way," said the leader.

And the slugs kept going. The world was still safe for humans, all because of Jimmy's and Robbie's big feet.

That wasn't very good.

Dead and badly injured slugs littered the battlefield. People walked knee-deep in slug guts. Budgies pecked at the dead and mutilated bodies. A dying slug handed his buddy his watch.

"Make sure my wife gets this," he said. "And tell the kids to do their homework every night."

"How many kids have you?" asked his friend.

"Four hundred and seventy-two."

"Will I tell them each individually, or will all together do?"

"Whatever," said the slug.

His eyes closed, and opened.

"It's a pity you don't have arms," he said. "Then I could have died in them."

"Ah, well," said his friend.

The slug's eyes closed, stayed closed, then opened.

"D'you know what?" he said. "I don't feel too bad now."

Boring.

Then a triplet stood on him.

CHAPTER NINE

Mean . . . .

while, Mister Mack walked into the bank, Kayla and Victoria were robbing a different bank.

Really?

No. Kayla and Victoria were robbing the supermarket, but that's a very different story.

What did they rob?

I don't have time to tell you, but it was delicious and the chocolate came off in the wash.

Mister Mack walked into the bank. It was full, but suddenly, there was plenty of space in front of him. He walked right up to the woman behind the counter.

"Good morning," said Mister Mack. The woman didn't answer.

"That's a bit rude," said Mister Mack to himself.

And he noticed something. Her hands were sticking up in the air. Mister Mack looked around. More people had their hands in the air. In fact, everybody had their hands in the air.

"Aha," said Mister Mack to himself.

"It must be stick-your-hands-up-in-the-air day. For charity."

"I want to talk to the manager, please," said Mister Mack to the woman behind the counter.

He held up the saw.

"I think he'll give me some money when he sees this," he said. "What do you think?"

"Yes," said the woman.

"How much do you think he'll give me?" said Mister Mack.

"As much as you want," said the woman.

"Great," said Mister Mack. "It'll be easier than I thought. Will he talk to me, do you think?"

"I'm sure he will."

"Great," said Mister Mack. "Because the last time I asked him for money, he told me to get lost and to stay out of his bank."

"I don't think he'll say that this time," said the woman.

"Great," said Mister Mack. "I told him I had an idea that would kill him. But I don't think he was listening."

Robbie and Jimmy saw the manager, Mister Meaney, come out of his office behind the counter. And they heard a siren. And another siren. And more sirens.

"There must be a fire somewhere," said Mister Mack.

"Yes," said the woman behind the counter.

Mister Meaney walked slowly to the counter.

"Good morning, Mister Eh —"

"Mack," said Mister Mack.

"Ah yes," said Mister Meaney. "Good morning, Mister Mack."

"Good morning, Mister Meaney," said Mister Mack.

He pointed the saw at Mister Meaney, and Mister Meaney put his hands in the air. The sirens outside got louder and louder.

"Mister Mack," said Mister Meaney. "Please, put the gun down."

"What gun?" said Mister Mack. "Have you any wood in here that you want cut?"

"I don't think so," said Mister Meaney.

"Actually," said another voice behind the counter.

They looked, and saw a small man at a big desk, with his hands way up.

"Actually, Mister Meaney," said the man. "You promised me that you'd get someone to cut a few inches off the legs of this desk because I can't reach my mouse without standing up."

Mister Meaney stared at the man.

"Mister O'Dim," he said. "This is hardly the time to—"

But Mister Mack put the saw up to his shoulder.

"No problem," he said.

Some people screamed and one or two fainted but, when the sawdust cleared, they all saw: the desk was exactly three inches closer to the floor. Mister Mack had done a perfect job.

"Impressed?" said Mister Mack.

"Gulp," said Mister Meaney. "Yes."

"My mouse!" said the man at the desk.

His sandwiches were shredded, all over the floor, his shoelaces were singed and smoking, but he didn't seem to mind.

"Come here, ickle mousey!"

Then they heard a loud voice from outside.

"This is the Garda. Put your hands up."

And Mister Mack put the saw on the counter and lifted his hands into the air. It was keep-your-hands-up-in-the-air day, and he didn't want to spoil the fun.

Jimmy and Robbie heard the door behind them open and they felt the air rush past them, followed by two

Guards, and another two Guards. The bank was suddenly full of Guards.

"Excuse me, Sergeant."

"Get off my foot, Sergeant."

"Oh, I beg your pardon, Sergeant."

The big backs of the Guards got in Jimmy's and Robbie's way and they couldn't see Mister Mack. Then, like two big doors, two big Garda backs moved apart and more Guards came toward Robbie and Jimmy, and Mister Mack was in the middle of them, like the figs in one of his fig-rolls.

He smiled at the boys but he looked worried.

"Tell your mammy," he said over the Garda shoulders.

"Tell her what?" said Robbie.

"I'm not sure," said Mister Mack.

The Garda fig-roll was at the door by now.

"Something about me being in trouble," said Mister Mack. "But I don't know why."

He was gone. And most of the Garda backs were gone. Robbie and Jimmy could see the door and, through the door, they could see two huge Guards closing the doors of a big black van.

"What'll we do now?" said Jimmy.

"We'd better tell Mammy," said Robbie.

"OK," said Jimmy.

They saw Mister Mack's face pressed to the glass of the van door. He saw them and smiled as the van moved away slowly.

"But where is she?"

It had been a day full of problems so far, and this was easily the biggest one, so far. The boys' mother was Billie Jean, and they had no idea where she was.

CHAPTER TEN

Meanwhile . . .

Kayla and Victoria were sitting on a wall, eating chocolate things they'd borrowed from the supermarket.

A black Garda van passed.

"Batteries included," said Victoria.

"Who are you!" Kayla shouted.

"Who are you!"

Here's what they meant:

"Will you look at the head on that eejit in the back of the Garda van," said Victoria.

"That's no eejit!" Kayla shouted. "That's my dad!"

They jumped off the wall and hopped on to the bike. But before they could cycle after the Garda van, someone pulled Kayla's jumper and someone else pulled Victoria's. The bike went off by itself.

Robbie and Jimmy held Kayla and Victoria up in the air.

"Do you know where Mammy is?" asked Jimmy.

"Who are you!"

"No idea at all?" asked Robbie.

"Who are you!"

"Maybe America!"

"Who are you!"

"Maybe China! We'll never find her."

CHAPTER ELEVEN

Where was their mother?

The answer is easy but not very helpful.

She could have been anywhere.

What? Like a ghost?

No. Nothing like a ghost. Let me explain.

A week after he walked out of the biscuit factory, Mister Mack and Billie Jean Fleetwood-Mack were getting the dinner ready.

Boring.

They were killing a cow in the back garden. There were moos and blood all over the place.

Really?

No. They were in the kitchen. Billie Jean was peeling the spuds.

"Don't!" yelled a spud. "There's a zip at the back!"

But Billie Jean didn't hear him. She was talking to Mister Mack.

"I was thinking," said Billie Jean.

"You want to break another record," said Mister Mack.

"Yes," said Billie Jean.

Billie Jean was an amazing woman. She'd broken all kinds of records. She was the first woman in the world to climb the Spire, in Dublin. She was the fastest person to climb the Eiffel Tower, in Paris. She was the only woman to straighten the Leaning Tower, in Pisa. She'd made and broken all kinds of records. Second woman to cycle up Mount Everest.

Fastest woman to cycle down Mount Everest. First person to drive a tractor through the National Art Gallery. First woman to break into Mountjoy Jail. There were seven pages of the *Guinness Book of World Records* filled with Billie Jean's records, and that was a record too. Billie Jean couldn't go out the door without breaking a record. Fastest woman ever to cut the grass. She couldn't even go to the door without breaking a record.

First woman ever to bring the milk from the step to the kitchen on a skateboard. Records broke whenever she went near them.

And that was the problem.

Billie Jean was tired of breaking the easy records and she'd decided to go for the big one. She told Mister Mack.

Mister Mack looked at Billie Jean. God, he loved her. If his love could have been measured, it would have been a record – the most love ever felt for an Irishwoman. Billie Jean smiled at him, and Mister Mack broke his own record.

"How long will it take?" he asked.

"It's hard to say," she said. "Eight months, maybe."

"That's a long time," said Mister Mack. "You don't have to walk, do you?"

"No," said Billie Jean. "Any way I like, as long as I don't tell anyone."

"Except me," said Mister Mack.

"That's right," said Billie Jean. "That's the rule."

"I hope I don't blab," said Mister Mack.

"I'm sure you won't," said Billie Jean.

"Because if I do, there's no record. Isn't that right?"

"Yes," said Billie Jean. "But you won't."

Hey.

Yes.

What's going on? What's the record they're talking about?

Good question. But I can't answer it yet.

Why not?

I haven't made it up yet.

Really?

No. I have made it up. But I won't tell you yet, because it's more exciting that way.

No, it isn't.

Shut up.

CHAPTER TWELVE

Meanwhile, Mister Mack was in the police station. He was in a cell, and there were two detectives with him. One of the detectives was nice, and the other one wasn't nice at all. (One of them sweated a lot and smoked cigarettes. Can you guess which one? The answer is coming up.)

"Where's your wife, Mack?" said Not-Nice.

"I'm not telling you," said Mister Mack.

"Why not?" said Not-Nice.

"I just won't," said Mister Mack. "I can't."

"Why not?" said Not-Nice.

"Isn't the weather great for this time of year?" said Nice.

"It's a secret," said Mister Mack.

Not-Nice stared at Mister Mack.

"What age are you, Mack?" he said.

"Thirty-seven," said Mister Mack.

"You don't look a day over thirty," said Nice.

"Thank you," said Mister Mack. "I try to look after myself."

"You're looking at ten years behind bars, Mack," said Not-Nice. "How does that sound?"

"Shocking," said Nice. He lit his cigarette and wiped the sweat from his face.

"So," said Not-Nice. "Where's your wife? She could tell us if that gun's really a saw. Where is she?"

"I'm not telling," said Mister Mack.

CHAPTER THIRTEEN

Meanwhile, Billie Jean Fleetwood-Mack looked up at the blue sky.

"Ah," she said. "This is the life."

Billie Jean was on a raft, somewhere on the Pacific Ocean.

Kayla had been kind of right. Billie Jean was in, maybe, America, and in, maybe, China. She was in between them, floating on the ocean.

The sea was calm. The waves were being very nice, lifting the raft and shoving it gently towards –

she hoped – China. Billie Jean had just had her dinner, a tin of beans. She'd enjoyed it, but it had reminded her a lot of the dinner she'd had the day before, and the day before that. Billie Jean had had a tin of beans every day since she'd climbed on to the raft and pushed it away from the California shore, twenty-four days before. She farted a lot but she didn't mind that, because every fart pushed the raft a few inches closer to – she really hoped – China. But beans were beans – they were boring little lads.

Billie Jean looked up at the sky again.

"Ah," she said, again. "This really is the life."

But she didn't think that this was the life at all. In fact, Billie Jean was bored and lonely. The first part of the trip had been great, across the Atlantic: storms and icebergs and other great stuff. Billie Jean had loved it. The raft fell apart, and she put it back together again, just before a shark ate the hammer and most of the nails. The journey across the United States was great, too, except people kept asking where she was going. And she couldn't tell them. It was against the rules.

"Hey! You're Irish. Where are you going?"

Here are some of Billie Jean's answers:

1. "The shops."
2. "My granny's."
3. "Eh."
4. "Mind your own business."

She was happy when she got to California and built a new raft. And now, here she was. Somewhere in—

On.

On the Pacific. Heading very slowly towards – oh God, she hoped – China. The sea was very calm, she hadn't seen a killer whale in ages, the sky was huge and blue.

Boring.

Billie Jean agreed. It *was* boring.

Then she saw something. In the distance. Land. She wasn't sure. She stared and stared. She looked away, and looked. And she saw – mountains.

Billie Jean ate the rest of her beans. Then she looked at the mountains and farted. The mountains got a tiny bit nearer. She farted again. The

mountains seemed nearer again. She farted all day and all night, even in her sleep. She slept and farted right through the next day, and when she woke up, the bottom of the raft was rubbing sand. Billie Jean was only a few feet from the shore.

She stepped out of the raft. The water was warm. It was a long beach and, before her, trees rose up into the mountains. She looked all around her. It was getting dark. She could see no houses, no boats, no one.

Then, something in the distance caught her eye. Further down the beach, a woman climbed out of a raft, walked to the shore, just like Billie Jean had done. Billie Jean ran to meet her.

"Hi," said Billie Jean.

"Hi," said the woman.

"Where are we?" asked Billie Jean.

"I'm not sure," said the woman. "Maybe China."

They suddenly looked at each other, very carefully. They were both Irish, and very far from home. They were both dressed for travel and adventure. They both looked like women who ran into strong wind and jumped off high things. They both farted at the exact same time, and they knew: they were both going after the same record – first woman to go around the world without telling anyone.

Hang on. She told Mister Mack.

You're allowed to tell just one person before you start.

That's stupid.

No, it isn't. If you tell one person, it proves that you really went off to break the record and that it wasn't just an accident or a coincidence.

The two women looked at each other.

"Seeyeh," said Billie Jean.

She started running.

CHAPTER FOURTEEN

Meanwhile, the Mack kids and Victoria were at home in the kitchen, eating their breakfast: maple syrup straight out of the bottle. It was the morning after Mister Mack had been arrested. The kids had all slept together in their parents' big bed.

Boring.

I agree. The kids were having a meeting.

"How do you know Mammy's going around the world?" asked Jimmy.

"Who are you."

"You were under the table when she told Dad?"

Kayla nodded.

"Why do you think she's in China?" asked Robbie.

Kayla shrugged.

"Who are you."

"Because she left a month ago, and that's how long it would take you to get to China if you went west, across the Atlantic Ocean, the United States and the Pacific?"

Kayla nodded.

"We'll need Rover," said Jimmy.

Kayla nodded. And so did Victoria.
They were ready to go.

CHAPTER FIFTEEN

But Rover wasn't.

"China?" he said. "You're jesting."

They were in Rover's shed. Rover was lying on his rug, reading the greyhound racing results.

To adults, Rover was the standard dog. He barked, he pooed, he sometimes growled. He scratched on the door when he wanted to get out, and he whined when he wanted to come back in. He did clever things too. He went to the shop and brought home his owner's newspaper, in his mouth. But what his owner didn't know was, Rover always stopped and read the paper on the way home. His owner often looked at his phone bill and gasped.

"Janey, Rover," he'd say. "I don't remember making all those calls."

He didn't make the calls. Rover did.

"Woof," Rover would say, and wag his tail.

While his owner slept or went to work, Rover ran several successful businesses. He supplied poo to the Gigglers, who made grown-ups who'd been mean to children stand on it. He ran a dog talent agency. All those dogs you see on the telly,

Rover supplied them all. All those dogs who do funny, cute things in the home video programmes – they were all Rover's. They hated the work. "It's so humiliating, darling."

But the money was good, and ten per cent of it was Rover's. The puppy that runs through the house in the toilet paper ad – he was a Rover client. That dog in the Bus Eireann ad, the red setter that runs beside the bus – he was another one of Rover's.

INTERESTING INFORMATION:

"Bus Eireann" means "Irish Bus". It's a bus company. The funny thing is, though, the red setter in the Bus Eireann ad isn't Irish at all. His name is Tibor, and he comes from Hungary. Back to Rover and the story.

And that wasn't all. Hey, adult, if you're reading this book with a kid: did you ever answer your phone and hear a voice:

"Good morning. Do you mind if I ask you some questions? It will only take ten minutes of your time."

That was probably Rover you were talking to.

"Are you happy with your bank?"

Probably Rover.

"Have you thought about insurance?"

Probably Rover.

"How's it going, pal. Would you be interested in a leather jacket?"

Definitely Rover.

Rover could sell anything. He even sold Germany once, over the phone, to a man in Ringsend.

"D'you want it delivered, or will you collect?"

"Delivered," said the man.

"No problem," said Rover. "And I'll tell you what. We'll throw in Austria for an extra ten euro. How does that sound?"

"Lovely."

But that was years ago. Rover was older now, and taking it easy.

"China?" he said. "You're jesting."

He waited for them to go.

"Ah, come on, Rover."

"You can do it."

"Who are you?"

"Please, Rover."

"Batteries included."

Rover looked at them over his reading glasses.

"Get lost," he said. "I've retired."

"What age are you?" asked Jimmy.

"Ten," said Rover.

"That's not old enough to retire," said Robbie.

"I'm seventy if you convert it into dog years," said Rover.

"That's not that old," said Robbie.

"Eighty-nine if you convert it into euros," said Rover.

"That's still not that old," said Robbie. "Our granny's ninety, and she plays for Shamrock Rovers."

"I've seen her play," said Rover. "Believe me, she's old."

He got back to the racing results.

"So, you won't help us find our mammy?" asked Robbie.

Rover didn't answer.

"So, you'll let the orphan catcher take us away and throw us into an orphanage?" asked Jimmy.

Then Kayla said something in a tiny, tearful voice. And she held out her little hands.

"Who are you?"

Rover stood up.

"OK, OK. You win."

Here is what Kayla actually said:

"Please, sir, can I have some more?"

INTERESTING INFORMATION:

Kayla was a brilliant impressionist. She had just done her Oliver Twist impression for Rover. She could also do impressions of the following people: Eminem, Beyoncé, Nelson Mandela, the Hulk and Scooby-Doo.

"OK, OK," said Rover. "You win. When do we start?"

"Batteries included!"

And Victoria and Kayla jumped on to his back.

"Now?" said Rover. "Well, I'll have to go to the toilet first. The ol' bladder isn't what it used to be. Get off me."

"Who are you?"

"No, I can't go while I'm running. Get off."

CHAPTER SIXTEEN

Meanwhile, Billie Jean was running around Beijing, the biggest city in China – the first woman ever to bypass Beijing. She had planned on walking into Beijing and staying a few days. But, now, she couldn't do that.

She looked over her shoulder.

The other woman was still there, right behind her, the exact same distance.

Billie Jean kept running.

THE DAILY OUTRAGE

BANK ROBBER HAS TERRIFIED NEIGHBOURS FOR YEARS,

by Our Staff Reporter, Paddy Hackery.

Crazed bank robber Mister Mack is a dangerous man, according to his neighbours.

"I saw him cough once," said a woman who did not want to be named. "And he didn't even put his hand to his mouth. He nearly killed the lot of us."

Every house has a story to tell.

"He once shouted 'Nice day' at me, and it wasn't a nice day at all. It was horrible."

"He once helped me across the street," said an elderly neighbour. "And I didn't want to cross the street. I was stuck on the wrong side for four days, all because of him."

"He's a bit of a weirdo," said a local shopkeeper. "He doesn't even have a first name."

Mister Mack looked up from the newspaper.

"I do so have a first name," he said. "It's Mister."

THE STORY OF HOW MISTER MACK GOT HIS FIRST NAME

Jimmy and Robbie's teacher was called Mister Eejit. He got that name when a man came cycling down the street checking all the names of the people who lived in the different houses. Mister Eejit's father was building the house, and he was holding a concrete block when the man got off his bike. "What is your name?" said the man at the exact same time that Mister Eejit's father let the block slip out of his fingers. The block smashed his toes as the man said "name" and Mister Eejit's father yelled, "Eejit!" giving out to himself for dropping the block. By the time Mister Eejit's father had nursed and kissed his poor tootsies, the man was cycling away. "My name's O'Malley!" he shouted. But it was too late. His name was now Eejit, and so was his son's, Robbie and Jimmy's teacher.

Meanwhile, the man cycled around the corner and stopped at the next house. Mister Mack's mother and father lived there. The man got off his bike and rang the bell. Mister Mack's father opened the door. He looked very happy and tired. "What is your name?" said the man. "Anthony Mack," said Mister Mack's father. "And does anyone else live here?" said the man. "Yes," said Mister Mack's father. "Name?" said the man. "Mary Margaret Mooney-Mack," said Mister Mack's father. "Any children?" asked the man. And this was why Mister Mack's father looked so happy and tired. Mister Mack had been born the night before. Mister Mack's father had just come home from the hospital. "Oh, yes," he said proudly. "A boy." "Name?" said the man. And here was the problem. Mister Mack's parents hadn't thought of a name yet. Mister Mack's father looked at the man. "Well," he said. "I don't know, eh, Mister, eh. . ." "Mister," said the man, and he wrote it down. He got back on his bike. "A strange name," he said. "But we live in very strange times." "But," said Mister Mack's father. But it was too late. The man had cycled away. Mister Mack's father met his new neighbour at the gate. "My son's name is Mister," he said. "That's nothing," said his neighbour. "My son's name is Eejit." And that's a true story.

Mister Mack threw the newspaper on to the floor of his cell. He didn't want to read it any more.

The door opened, and the two detectives walked in.

"Good morning, Mister Mack," said Nice. "Have you had your breakfast?"

"Tell us about the gun, Mack," said Not-Nice.

"No," said Mister Mack.

"No, you won't tell us about the gun?"

"No, I haven't had my breakfast. And it isn't a gun. It's a saw."

"Here we go again," said Not-Nice. "What did you saw with it, Mack?"

"What would you like, Mister Mack?" said Nice.

"Wood," said Mister Mack.

"For your breakfast?" said Nice.

"No," said Mister Mack. "It's what the saw was for. Cutting wood."

"Of course it was," said Nice. "Cornflakes?"

"I'm confused," said Mister Mack.

"You're guilty," said Not-Nice.

"Ah, leave the poor man alone," said Nice. "He hasn't had his breakfast yet."

"So, where's the famous Billie Jean, Mack?" said Not-Nice. "Why isn't she here to rescue you?"

Mister Mack closed his eyes.

PROBABLY CHAPTER SEVENTEEN

Meanwhile, Rover was ready to go.

"What kept you?" said Robbie. "You were in the toilet all night."

"You'll understand when you're older, pal," said Rover. "Are we ready?"

Kayla and Victoria jumped onto his back.

Here was the plan. Kayla, Victoria and Rover would run around the world and find Billie Jean.

"No sweat," said Rover.

Meanwhile, Robbie and Jimmy would stay in Dublin.

"Nice one," said Rover.

But they weren't going to hang around, waiting for a happy ending. They were going to dig a tunnel under the Garda station and rescue Mister Mack.

"I'm good at tunnels," said Rover. "They're my speciality."

"No," said Jimmy. "You find our mammy."

"Fair enough," said Rover.

"Who are you?" asked Kayla.

"The M50," said Rover. "The traffic shouldn't be too bad."

And they were gone. Just like that, they were out of Rover's garden, and Jimmy and Robbie were alone.

"Let's get the shovels," said Jimmy.

"OK," said Robbie. "But will we watch a bit a telly first?"

"OK," said Jimmy.

They went into their house.

DEFINITELY CHAPTER EIGHTEEN

Meanwhile, Billie Jean was running along the Great Wall of China.

Billie Jean looked behind. The other woman had caught up with her. Billie Jean tripped. She fell and landed on one of her knees.

"Ouch."

She looked, and saw the other woman run ahead. The woman turned as she ran.

"I'm sorry that happened," she shouted. "Do you want me to stop?"

Billie Jean waved.

"No," she shouted back. "I'll catch up with you."

"Oh no, you won't."

"We'll see about that," said Billie Jean quietly.

She took off her rucksack and opened it. She had some special medicines in the bag, and one of them was called Mendo-nee.

"I hope this stuff works," she said.

Meanwhile, Missis Meaney, the orphan catcher, was looking for the Mack kids. She was walking down their street, getting closer to the house. She was a nasty woman. She had a mole on her chin, and her clothes were too tight. Her shoes were loud, and she had a nasty laugh. She had a big net, a bigger bum, and a bad, bad temper. (Sinister fact: She was the bank manager's sister, and he

had told her that the Mack children were at home, all alone, without their parents.) She kicked the door open.

"Ha ha," she shouted. "Caught you!"

The family looked up from their breakfast.

"Wrong house, missis," said the father.

"Oh," she said.

"And you'll have to pay for that lock."

"Oh."

She tried hard to look nasty again. She sniffed the air.

"I smell orphans," she said.

"No, missis," said the father. "That's the toast. I burned it."

His children, all ten of them, laughed. The orphan catcher hated that sound. She ran out of the house. She was blushing and furious. She sniffed again.

"I'll show them," she said. "I *do* smell orphans."

She headed for the Mack house.

Meanwhile, the M50, the motorway that goes around Dublin, was blocked.

"Did you ever see anything like this traffic?" said Rover.

Meanwhile, the orphan catcher charged into the Mack house.

"Ha ha! Caught you!"

But no one was there. The house seemed empty. She heard voices and crept to the sitting room.

"They're watching telly," she said. "The lazy little messers."

She pushed the door.

"Ha ha."

But the room was empty. The telly was on, but no one was there. There was a film on, *The Great Escape*. She watched men digging a tunnel. Then the actor Steve McQueen came onto the screen. He was in a cell, throwing a baseball at the wall.

"Oh, I like him," she said, and she sat down to watch.

Meanwhile, Jimmy and Robbie were under the telly, digging a tunnel.

"I wonder what's on telly?" said Jimmy.

"Probably something boring," said Robbie.

Meanwhile, Mister Mack was alone in his cell. He was sitting on the floor, leaning against the wall.

"God, this is boring," he said. "I wish I had a baseball, like that fella in *The Great Escape*."

Then he saw something. A match. On the floor. The nice detective had dropped it. Mister Mack picked it up.

Meanwhile, Rover had kidnapped a motorbike. With Kayla behind him and Victoria on the handlebars, he drove through the traffic, and over it. Drivers screamed and fainted when they heard the noise on their roofs.

"What do you think you're doing?" a driver yelled.

"Looking for this kid's ma," said Rover. "Have a nice day."

They had just reached the Tallaght roundabout.

USEFUL INFORMATION:

The Tallaght roundabout is the only roundabout that can be seen from the Moon. We know this because a man from Tallaght called Ned Mullahy once went to the Moon, and he looked down and saw it. "Hey, lads," he said to the other astronauts. "There's the Tallaght roundabout. See? To the left of Kelly's shed."

Back to the story.

The cars and trucks in front of Rover went around the roundabout. But Rover drove straight on to it.

Was he taking a shortcut?

Yes, he was. But he didn't just drive across the grass, to get to the other side. In fact, he didn't drive across the roundabout at all. He drove into it. He disappeared. The bike, Kayla, Victoria, Rover – they all disappeared.

Rover knew all the world's shortcuts. He knew the little ones, like the quickest way from your house to the shop. And the bigger ones, like the quickest way to get from Dublin to Donegal. (HINT: Don't go through Argentina.) But that wasn't all. Rover knew all the secret shortcuts in the world. He knew a wardrobe in London that brought you straight to Narnia. He knew a secret railway platform in Euston Station, in London, that brought you straight to the Watermill, a pub in Raheny. And he knew a hole behind a bush in the middle of the Tallaght roundabout that brought you straight to –

"Who are you!"

"That's right, kid," said Rover. "Las Vegas."

He climbed off the motorbike. And,

for the first time that day, the motorbike spoke.

"Coo-il," he said. "Where's Elvis?"

And he drove off, into the lights and noise.

Meanwhile, Robbie and Jimmy were making progress. They'd tunnelled under ten houses, and across the street. But they were running out of wood to support the roof and stop the tunnel from caving in. So far, they'd used their bunk beds and the stairs to the attic. And they had to get rid of some of the muck before they could dig any further.

They crawled back under the sitting room. They could hear the telly.

"Crazed gunman, Mister Mack, remains in custody today. More in our news bulletin, after the movie."

Robbie climbed up, and out the back of the telly. There was no one in the sitting room. He whispered down to Jimmy.

"All clear."

Jimmy handed buckets of muck up to Robbie, and he emptied them out the window, into the garden.

Meanwhile, the orphan catcher was in the kitchen. She was making a jam-and-cornflake sandwich.

"War films always make me hungry," she said.

She stopped. She thought she'd heard something. She sniffed.

"Orphans," she said.

She picked up her net. She crept slowly to the sitting-room door. She jumped in.

"Ha ha!"

It was empty.

Meanwhile, Robbie had climbed out the sitting-room window and gone around to the kitchen door. He was hungry. He opened the door and saw the sandwich on the table.

Meanwhile, Jimmy was in the sitting room, inside the telly, looking out at the orphan catcher.

Meanwhile, Mister Mack had started to scrape the cement between the bricks of the cell wall, with the match.

The cement crumbled, and dust fell to the floor.

Meanwhile, Robbie picked up the sandwich and walked into the hall. He took a bite – yeuk – and came to the sitting room door.

"A warning to all kids!"

He saw Jimmy's face, pressed to the inside of the screen.

"Kids with sandwiches should never walk into sitting rooms!"

Robbie stopped.

"A government report just released advises all children to stay out of sitting rooms if they have sandwiches."

Robbie heard a voice.

"What's that rubbish?"

He heard a big bum slap down on the couch. He saw a big arm, and a hand holding the remote control, pointing at the telly. He saw Jimmy's face disappear.

Meanwhile, more cement fell to the

cell floor, and on to Mister Mack's bare feet.

Meanwhile, the orphan catcher went back into the kitchen. Her sandwich was there, where she'd left it. But there was a bite taken out of it. And there was something else, a piece of paper, beside the plate. She picked it up and read: "You make brutal sandwiches – ha ha. Signed: The Phantom Orphan."

Meanwhile, Robbie was back in the tunnel, with Jimmy. He'd climbed in the sitting-room window when the orphan catcher went back to the kitchen. They were digging really fast now, getting nearer and nearer to the Garda station.

Meanwhile, Billie Jean was catching up with the other woman. They had galloped into Mongolia and they were now halfway across the Gobi Desert.

"It's lovely, isn't it?" the other woman shouted back to Billie Jean.

"Gorgeous," Billie Jean shouted back.

Meanwhile, Rover and the girls were charging across the Mojave Desert. The sand and stones were hot, so Rover had to go dead fast so his feet wouldn't burn too badly.

"Ouch, ouch, ouch, ouch, ouch!"

Meanwhile, the writer decided to make a cup of coffee. He stood up and walked to his office door.

"Hey!" Rover shouted. "Come back here!"

The writer went back to his computer. He sat down and wrote this: Meanwhile, Rover and the kids had run across the Mojave Desert and were now running along a beach near Los Angeles.

"That's better," said Rover.

The weather was great, but not too hot. It was perfect hairy-dog weather. A nice breeze lifted the hair from Rover's eyes and made him look even more handsome and intelligent than usual. As he ran along the edge of the water of Rocka-Hound Beach, the only beach in the world specially for dogs—

"Good man," said Rover. "Keep going."

As Rover ran along the beach, through the breakwater, the canine beach-babes and beach-bums stepped back to admire him.

"Wow," they said. "Awesome."

Meanwhile, the writer got up from

his desk to make a cup of coffee.

"Fire away," said Rover as he galloped elegantly through the surf.

"Who are you?" asked Kayla.

"Shut up, you," said Rover. "I'm not showing off."

The writer went into the kitchen and filled the kettle with cold water. He brought the kettle over to the counter and plugged it in. While he waited for the kettle to boil, he wiped the counter with a damp cloth and—

Boring.

The kettle exploded, and the writer was thrown across the kitchen. He hit the door, and it smashed as he went through it. He landed in the garden. He lay there, unconscious, for three hours.

Meanwhile, Robbie and Jimmy kept digging but were making no progress. They didn't move forward and the bucket didn't fill, even though they kept throwing muck into it. And Billie

Jean noticed something. She was running faster than she'd ever run before, but the mountains in front were getting no nearer. Mister Mack noticed something too. The air around his face was full of cement dust and little brick bits, floating, not dropping. And Rover noticed something. The beach went on for ever – it seemed like that. Every time he looked, he saw the same dogs looking at him.

"Wow."

"Awesome."

"Wow."

"Awesome."

"Wow."

"Awesome."

He looked down at his paws. They were moving, but he wasn't going anywhere.

Meanwhile, the writer was still lying in the garden, still unconscious. It had started to rain.

"Hey, pal."

It was Rover. But the writer couldn't hear him because he was seriously injured and fighting for his life.

"Hey, pal. Wake up."

The rain continued to fall, but the writer couldn't feel it.

"Wake up!"

"I'm unconscious, Rover," said the writer.

"If you don't wake up quick, I'll go over there and bite the leg off you."

Suddenly, the writer woke up. He jumped to his feet.

"That was close," he said.

"Hurry up!"

The writer bravely ignored his aches and pains and ran back into the house. He decided not to bother with coffee—

"Wise move."

And he ran straight back to his office and jumped on to his swivel chair. A pain shot through his body, but he ignored it. Blood ran from his forehead, over his eyes, but he wiped it away with his sleeve. He looked at the screen. He rubbed his hands together, then started writing.

"Wow!"

"Awesome!"

Rover felt the ground under his feet again. He felt the water, and the wind in his fur. He was moving again, racing along the beach. The canine beach-babes swooned.

"Seeyis, girls," said Rover. "Duty calls."

And he was gone, galloping across the sands of Southern California.

"See this rabbit hole in front of us?" he said.

"Batteries included," said Victoria.

"Gopher hole, rabbit hole," said Rover. "I don't care what kind of a hole it is, as long as we fit. Next stop, Beijing!"

And Rover dived down the hole.

CHAPTER . . . WHAT CHAPTER IS IT?

The writer went back to check.

CHAPTER NINETEEN

It was later in the day, and Mister Mack was worried. He'd made a hole in the cell wall. It was only a small hole, but the not-nice detective was leaning right beside it.

"Well," said Not-Nice. "What have you been up to?"

Mister Mack gulped.

"Nothing much," he said.

"Been trying to escape?" said Not-Nice.

"Not really," said Mister Mack.

"Nobody ever escaped from this station," said Nice. "Do you know why?"

"Why?" said Mister Mack.

"It's brand-new," said Nice. "It only opened on Monday."

"Is that right?"

"That's right."

"Enough small talk," said Not-Nice.

He stepped away from the wall and sat in front of Mister Mack.

"What were you going to do with the money?"

"What money?" said Mister Mack.

"Come on. The money you were going to take from the bank."

"I wasn't going to take any. . ."

Those dots are there because Mister Mack didn't finish what he was going to say, because Not-Nice threw a newspaper on to the desk.

"You were going to run off and join your wife, wherever she's hiding. Weren't you?"

Mister Mack looked at the paper.

THE EVENING INSULT

WIFE OF BANK ROBBER GOES INTO HIDING

by Our Special Reporter, Mary O'Contrary

SHE'S EVEN SCARIER THAN HIM, SAY NEIGHBOURS

Billie Jean Fleetwood-Mack, wife of crazed bank robber Mister Mack, has gone into hiding, according to their neighbours.

"They were in it together," said a woman who did not want to be named. "She had all the latest gear. Trainers, tracksuits, crash helmets. The money had to come from somewhere."

"I saw her in the supermarket once," said another neighbour. "And she had enough food in her trolley to feed a family of five for three or four days. I always wondered where they got the money."

Ms Fleetwood-Mack has been terrifying the neighbours for years.

THE EVENING INSULT

ROBBER

WIFE OF BANK ROBBER GOES INTO HIDING SHE'S EVEN SCARIER THAN HIM SAY NEIGHBOURS...

"She dived off her roof once and landed in our wheely bin," said an elderly neighbour.

"I haven't been the same since. It's been much nicer here since she went on the run." But where is the record-breaking Ms Fleetwood-Mack?

"The attic," one neighbour suggested. "She was always up there."

"Somewhere sunny," said another. "That's where I'd go if I was a bank robber's molly."

READERS' POLL: Where do YOU think she is? Have YOUR say.

Mister Mack looked up from the newspaper.

"That's just silly," he said.

"Oh yeah?" said Not-Nice.

"Yeah."

"How silly?"

Mister Mack stuck out his tongue and crossed his eyes.

"That silly," he said.

"You're beginning to get on my nerves," said Not-Nice. "Where is she?"

"I don't. . ."

Those dots are there because Mister Mack didn't finish what he was going to say, because he'd been distracted. The nice detective had walked over to the wall and, now, he put his finger in the hole.

"Will you look at that," said Nice. "It's a disgrace, so it is. A brand-new wall with a hole like that."

He took a handkerchief out of his pocket and stuffed it into the hole.

"You'll catch your death with the draught coming through that hole," he said. "We'll have to get it fixed."

Mister Mack moaned. He'd spent hours making that hole.

"Why did you moan?" asked Not-Nice.

"No reason," said Mister Mack.

"Why?" said Not-Nice.

And Mister Mack decided to really annoy Not-Nice.

"That's for me to know and you to find out," he said.

"Aagh," said Not-Nice.

He walked out of the cell and slammed the door.

CHAPTER TWENTY

This Chapter Is Sponsored by Happy-Dig,
Makers of the World's Best
Shovels and Spades

Meanwhile, Robbie and Jimmy stopped digging. They'd just heard something, above them.

"That was a door," said Robbie.

"Yeah," said Jimmy.

"Dad," said Robbie.

And Jimmy nodded. The boys had grown up listening to doors slamming just like that one. It was a Mister Mack kind of slam.

But Mister Mack didn't slam the door.

That's true. But a Mister Mack slam was never the sound of a door being slammed by Mister Mack. A Mister Mack slam was the sound of a door being slammed by someone who had just been talking to Mister Mack. The boys knew the sound well, and they loved it. When they were much younger, playing with their toys on the floor, they'd hear a door slam and they'd look at each other.

"Da da?" one of them would say.

"Da da," the other would answer.

Mister Mack was a nice man, but something about him made people slam doors.

"Will we go to the pictures?" said Billie Jean, once.

"I'm sorting out my socks," said Mister Mack.

"But the film starts in ten minutes.

Can the socks not wait?"

Mister Mack picked up some of the odd socks.

"But the poor things are lonely," he said. "And I saw the film this afternoon. She runs off with the doctor, and the car chase isn't very good."

Slam!

He looked up. Billie Jean was gone, and the bedroom door was wobbling.

"Mister Mack?"

It was Mister Mack's boss in the biscuit factory.

"Yes?" said Mister Mack.

"Have you a minute?"

Mister Mack searched his pockets. He found two euro, a banana, his keys and one of Kayla's baby teeth.

"No," he said. "I don't have a minute. Sorry."

Slam!

Mother Teresa, of Calcutta, the most famous nun in the world, once called at the Mack house. Mister

Mack answered the door.

"Hello," he said. "You look familiar."

"Would you please give some money for the poor?" asked Mother Teresa.

"How do I know you won't waste it on drugs?" said Mister Mack.

Slam!

Mother Teresa was so angry, she beat up three teenagers and threw her mobile phone through the pet shop window.

"Tweet tweet!" said a budgie. "Is that who I think it is?"

"She must have met Mister – tweet tweet – Mack."

It got to the point where Mister Mack didn't even have to speak. He got that look on his face, and people slammed the door. Billie Jean slammed a door before she spoke to him, even if she was speaking to him on the phone.

"Abah, abah."

It was Kayla's idea. And it worked. Once she'd slammed the door, Billie Jean didn't mind what silly thing Mister Mack said or did. It became a joke. And he invented a special door for Billie Jean, for her birthday. It was on wheels so she could pull it wherever she went and always have a door to slam if she wasn't near a real one.

Anyway, it was a Mister Mack slam that the boys had just heard. Right over their heads.

They could see each other grinning in the dark.

CHAPTER TWENTY-ONE

This Chapter Is Sponsored by Christopher Byrne, Maker of Very Good Doors "Need a Door? Dial 555-6832 and Ask for Gisty"

Meanwhile, Billie Jean was running through Omsk, a city in Russia. The traffic was mad because people were going home from work. Drivers were honking and shrieking, and their cars were making a lot of noise too. But as Billie Jean ran past a block of flats, she heard a door slam.

"Oh dear," she said. "How I miss Mister Mack."

And she cried a little bit as she finally caught up with the other woman.

"Will we finish together?" said the other woman. "Side by side."

"We will not," said Billie Jean. "None of that women-together nonsense for me. I'm going to win."

And she ran ahead of the other woman.

"Cheerio."

CHAPTER TWENTY-TWO

**This Chapter Is Sponsored by
Bow-Wow-Spex,
Makers of Quality Glasses
and Contact Lenses
for Your Dog**

"Next stop, Beijing."

The last time we saw Rover and the girls, they had just jumped down a rabbit hole that had been made by a very big gopher. Now, the street light came charging in at them. Rover jumped out of the tunnel.

"Hello, Beijing!"

And there, in front of them, was the Spire. Rover put on his glasses.

"It looks like the one in Dublin," he said.

He looked at the people passing.

"And they don't look very Chinese."

"Who are you?" said Kayla.

"Who are you calling an eejit?" said Rover.

But he had to admit it. They were back in Dublin, on O'Connell Street, thousands of miles from where he'd expected them to be.

"Excellent," said Rover. "It's all going to plan. Come on."

He started running.

But he only ran ten yards, and stopped.

"It's no good, girls," said Rover. "Poor ol' Rover's flummoxed. What'll we do?"

CHAPTER TWENTY-THREE

This Chapter Is Sponsored by
Keep-'Em-In,
Makers of Secure Prisons
and Play-Schools

Mister Mack sat in his cell. The slam was the only other thing in the cell, and it was dying.

Poor Mister Mack. Tomorrow morning they'd be coming to take him to court. And, after that, he'd be all alone for years. In a cell. In a prison. He knew Billie Jean could have saved him. But she was thousands of miles away. A tear crawled out of his eye and rolled down his cheek. He was so unhappy.

How unhappy?

Do you have a dog?

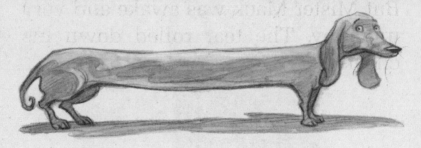

Yeah.

What's its name?

Noodles.

Well, Noodles died this morning.

Oh no!

Are you unhappy?

Yeah.

Well, Mister Mack was even unhappier. The tear rolled down his cheek and—

I want Noodles.

I'll tell you what. If you promise not to interrupt again, Noodles might just come back to life.

Really?

Promise?

Promise.

Noodles isn't dead. He's just asleep. But Mister Mack was awake and very unhappy. The tear rolled down his cheek.

Then he heard something. A knock on the floor.

Meanwhile, Kayla and Victoria explained the plan to Rover.

"Who are you?"

"Batteries included."

"Who are YOU?"

"Batteries included and included and included and batteries!"

"Fair enough," said Rover.

"Included!"

What does all that mean?

Meanwhile, a little dog called Noodles ran out into the middle of O'Connell Street, right in front of a bus and—

Sorry, sorry, I forgot.

Luckily, the bus wasn't moving. Noodles jumped back on to the path. He passed a dog called Rover.

"How's it going, Rover?"

"Not too bad, Noodles."

"So," said Rover. "Where now?"

"Who are you."

"The airport!? But I know a shortcut."

"Who *are* you."

"OK, OK. The airport."

And Rover ran up Dorset Street.

Here was Kayla and Victoria's plan. Instead of chasing after Billie Jean, they'd go in the other direction and catch her coming the other way. Billie Jean had left Ireland and travelled west, across the Atlantic Ocean and America. Rover and the girls had tried to catch up with her. But now, they'd go in the opposite direction, east. With a bit of luck, they'd meet her on her way back, because the world is round. And if you go one way, you'll always come back the other way, even if it feels like you're still going the same way.

Meanwhile, Mister Mack watched the tear that had rolled down his cheek. He'd just heard something. A knock on the floor. The tear hit the floor and bounced right back up into his eye. The eye was surprised, and so was Mister Mack. And the knocking continued. Mister Mack put his ear to the floor. He heard a soft knock.

He moved his ear, and the knocking was louder. He moved again – louder. Again – very loud. Again, and the floor whacked his ear.

"Ouch," said Mister Mack.

"Dad?" said the floor.

Meanwhile, a plane called EI 787 was about to take off, going to Frankfurt, a city in Germany.

"That's a lovely starry sky up there," said EI 787, to himself. "Oh oh, here's the end of the runway. I'd better get up. One. Two – ah!"

EI 787 had just felt Rover's teeth.

As the wheels left the ground, Rover jumped and bit one of them. And he hung on, as EI 787 flew over Dublin Bay, higher and higher, and then Victoria and Kayla scrambled off Rover's back. They climbed to the top of the big wheel. They had a great view from up there – the necklace of lights around the bay, Bull Island, the mountains.

"Who are you!"

Kayla pointed.

"That's right, kid," said Rover as he climbed up beside them. "That's the poo I did this morning. I'm not sure why, but I am kind of proud of it."

They could see it under a streetlight.

"Batteries included."

"Thanks," said Rover. "The Gigglers will love that one."

The wheel started moving, rising slowly into the plane.

"Hang on," said Rover.

They saw no more of Dublin as they were lifted into EI 787.

"It's going to be cold," said Rover. "Really, really freezing."

Kayla and Victoria pulled up their hoods.

"That's grand," said Rover.

Meanwhile, Mister Mack said nothing. He'd never spoken to a floor before, but then, a floor had never called him Dad before. He stopped looking at the floor.

But it did it again.

"Dad?"

Mister Mack looked at the walls and the ceiling.

"Dad?!"

He looked at the door.

"Dad??!!!"

He gave up.

"I'm sorry," he said. "But I'm not your dad."

"Dad!!!??? It's Jimmy!"

"Jimmy?"

"Dad?"

"Is that you, Jimmy?"

"Yes."

"Dad!"

"And Robbie?"

"Hi."

And Mister Mack knew.

"You've come to rescue me."

The tear that had jumped back into his eye climbed back out again.

Meanwhile, Billie Jean had crossed

the border into Poland. She was happy, and feeling happier with every step. She was nearly home. Just Poland, Germany, Holland, a quick swim across the North Sea, across England, another swim, and she'd be there. Back home to her family. She was dying to see them again, to hug and cuddle them. And she'd be the winner, the first woman ever to go around the world without telling anyone.

She ran through miles and miles of wheat. Wheat, wheat and more of it, swaying in the gentle evening breeze.

But the breeze was suddenly stronger, and the other woman flew past Billie Jean. Billie Jean tried to keep up.

"How come you can suddenly run so fast?" she shouted.

"I'm allergic to wheat," the woman shouted back. "Ha ha."

I wish I was, thought Billie Jean as she watched the other woman disappear into the dust and the darkness.

But Billie Jean was allergic to only one thing: Irish music. But there was no Irish music in Poland, so she couldn't keep up with the woman. She couldn't even see her any more.

Meanwhile, the orphan catcher – remember her? – was trying to fix the telly.

"Where's Steve McQueen?" she asked.

She looked behind the telly and saw the hole.

"Ha ha," she said. "Just as I thought."

She started to climb down.

Meanwhile, Mister Mack was scraping the cement between the floor tiles with his fingernail. He could hear the boys below him scraping too.

"Is Kayla with you?" he asked.

"No," said Jimmy. "She's gone looking for Mammy."

"Oh fine," said Mister Mack. "Just as long as she's not in any trouble."

Meanwhile, Kayla was dangling from the wheel as EI 787 prepared to land at Frankfurt Airport. Victoria was beside her. Rover was upside down, clinging to the wheel.

They'd been busy during the flight. They'd opened most of the suitcases in the plane, looking for clothes that would make good parachutes. As the wheels were lowered, all the clothes from the suitcases poured out of the plane. Trousers, shirts, socks, knickers, shoes. They all fell out of EI 787 and dropped slowly through the night to the ground.

"Right," said Rover. "I'm getting bored up here. Let's get going."

Kayla and Victoria slid down the wheel – the plane was 10,000 feet above the ground – and grabbed Rover's fur.

"That's right," said Rover. "Give us a scratch while you're at it."

They held on to Rover's back.

"Ready?" said Rover.

"Who are you?"

And Rover jumped.

Meanwhile, Billie Jean had run across the border into Germany. But she couldn't see the other woman. There was no wheat now, but the woman must have been miles ahead.

"I'll never catch her," said Billie Jean.

She was beginning to feel very tired.

Meanwhile, the orphan catcher was crawling through the tunnel. She stopped, and sniffed.

"I can smell them," she said. "The little orphans."

Meanwhile, Mister Mack's fingernail felt something. Another fingernail. And soon the cement began to drop away and Mister Mack could see his children's fingers.

Under the tile, Robbie and Jimmy got ready and pushed the tile. The first thing they saw was Mister Mack's nose.

"Hi, Dad."

"Hi, boys," said the nose.

Meanwhile, Rover was falling to Germany. He was surrounded by shirts and blouses, vests and bras and waistcoats. Kayla and Victoria had rucksacks on their backs.

"OK," said Rover. "Fire away."

Kayla opened the zip of her rucksack, and a big beautiful dress flew out and filled up with air.

"Batteries included!"

At the same time, Victoria did the

same thing. Her dress filled with air, and the two little girls shot back up. Rover went with them, because they were holding tight to his fur. They shot right past EI 787's nose.

"There go two girls on a dog," said the pilot.

"Yeah yeah yeah," said the co-pilot. "The sky is full of them at this time of night."

Meanwhile, the boys climbed up into Mister Mack's cell.

And meanwhile, the orphan catcher was getting closer and closer.

And meanwhile, a German boy called Klaus was in trouble. He was late for his dinner and he'd lost one of his shoes. He knew his mother would be annoyed. He was always losing his shoes. He was walking home now, very slowly. This is what he sounded like: stomp, slap, stomp, slap, stomp, slap. Suddenly, a shoe hit him on the head. It had fallen 10,000 feet, so it hurt.

But before he realized that he was in great pain, he saw that the shoe was the

exact same as the one he'd lost. The pain ran away, and Klaus looked up. He saw a dog and two girls sailing over his head. "*Danke,*" he shouted.

"No problem, *mein Herr,*" the dog shouted back.

Meanwhile, a very fast woman ran past Klaus. And Rover saw her.

"There's a fast woman down there, look. God, she's a flyer. She must be Irish."

The girls looked, but it wasn't Billie Jean.

"Keep your eyes peeled," said Rover.

Meanwhile, Mister Mack hugged the boys.

"Let's go," said Robbie.

"Where?" said Mister Mack.

"Back down," said Jimmy. "Out of here. Home."

"Ah yes," said Mister Mack. "But, you know, I was making a hole in the wall over there. It seems a shame to waste it."

"Come on, Dad," said Robbie.

He knew how to move his father.

"There are fig-rolls in the kitchen."

And Mister Mack jumped into the hole.

Meanwhile, Billie Jean was running across a bridge. The bridge crossed the River Main, but Billie Jean didn't notice the river or the lights that shone on the water. There were two reasons for this: she was very tired. And Rover landed on her.

Billie Jean and Rover spun in the air, and this was lucky for Billie Jean

because she landed on Rover. The two dresses landed on her, followed by the two girls. Rover decided that the time had come to break his rule about talking in front of adults.

"Get off," he said.

Billie Jean pulled the dresses off her head.

"Who are you?" said Kayla.

"Kayla!" said Billie Jean.

"Batteries included!"

"And Victoria!" said Billie Jean. "What are you doing here? You must tell me everything."

"I said get off," said Rover.

Billie Jean looked down and saw that she was sitting on fur.

"Hurry up!"

Talking fur.

She jumped off Rover, and Rover stood up.

"About time," he said.

He looked at Billie Jean as he shook off the German dust.

"Our little secret, yeah?"

"OK," said Billie Jean.

"Woof," said Rover.

And Kayla and Victoria told Billie Jean all about it.

"Who are you."

"Batteries included."

"Who are you."

"Batteries included."

"Oh my God," said Billie Jean.

"Who are you."

"Batteries, batteries, batteries."

"Who are you-ooooooo!"

"Oh my —"

"Included, included."

"God."

"Included."

"He's in prison?" asked Billie Jean.

"A guest of the nation," said Rover.

"But how will we get home? I'm exhausted."

"Don't look at me, missis," said Rover.

Meanwhile, Mister Mack followed

the boys as they crawled back through the tunnel.

Meanwhile, the orphan catcher had muck in her eyes. She rubbed them and saw a boy's face right in front of her. She screamed, and heard a voice.

"Back! Back!"

A boy's voice.

"Ha ha," she said. "Got you."

Meanwhile, a boy called Klaus was feeling happy as he walked past Rover, the girls and Billie Jean. He had two shoes, and was looking forward to his dinner.

He heard the accents. He stopped walking.

"You are Irish?" he asked.

"Who are you?" said Kayla.

"I love Ireland," said Klaus. "Especially much I like your Irish muuu-zic."

And he started singing.

"TIM REILLY WAS A HANDSOME LAD, WHO LOVED TO JUMP AND CLIMB —"

Klaus kept singing.

WARNING:

Irish music is a killer and should be approached very carefully. Always wear rubber gloves when close to Irish music. Never turn your back on Irish music and never, ever listen to it. Back to the story.

"AND HE DIED FOR DEAR OLD IRELAND TWENTY-SEVEN TIMES."

Billie Jean screamed. She grabbed Kayla, Victoria and Rover and she ran. She had to get away from the Irish music.

Rover put his paws around Billie Jean's neck and held on tight.

"I could get used to this," said Rover.

Meanwhile, Mister Mack climbed back into his cell. The boys followed him. They put the tile over the hole.

Meanwhile, Billie Jean ran through Cologne, with two girls and a dog on her back. She was slowing down, but

she could see the other woman just ahead of her.

"We're Irish!" she shouted.

A man stopped walking.

"Irish?" he said. "Oh, I love the Irish muuuu-zic."

And he started to sing.

"ME NAME IS PATSY GRADY –

AND I WORK FOR MICROSOFT –"

Billie Jean screamed, and ran past the other woman.

"Keep in touch," said Rover. "Head west," he told Billie Jean. "I know a shortcut."

"We're Irish," roared Billie Jean.

"Irish?" said another man. "We love very much the Irish muuu-zic."

He sang.

"WALT DISNEY WAS AN IRISH LAD –

HE CAME FROM BALLYMUCK –"

And Billie Jean ran.

"HE WALKED ALL DAY,
          TO AMERICAY –
WITH HIS GOOD FRIEND, DÓNAL DUCK."

Meanwhile, the orphan catcher bashed her head on the tile.

And meanwhile, Rover put on his glasses, then pointed to a tree.

"Over there."

"I'm exhausted," said Billie Jean. "I need a rest."

And the dog sang.

"I'VE BEEN A WILD ROVER FOR MANY A
          YEAR-RRRR –
AND I SPENT ALL MY MONEY ON
WHISKEY AND BEE-EEER –"

He sang right into Billie Jean's ear. She dashed to the tree and jumped down the hole behind it.

Meanwhile, Not-Nice opened the cell door. He stared at Robbie and Jimmy.

"Who are you?"

The floor tile rose slowly, with the orphan catcher's mucky head right under it.

"Who are you?"

"Who are you?"

And Nice walked into the cell.

"Who are you?"

"Who are you?"

"Who are you?"

"How long now?" asked Billie Jean.

"Who are you," said Kayla.

"AND IT'S NO – NAY – NEVER-RRRR –

NO – NAY – NEVER NO MORE-

RRRRRRRRRR –"

Billie Jean charged through the darkness.

The orphan catcher grabbed Jimmy and Robbie. She held their ankles and pulled them towards the hole.

"WILL I –

PLAY-YYYYYY

THE WILD ROVER-RRRRRRR –"

Mister Mack grabbed the boys' hands.
"Who are you?" he shouted.
"Who are you?" the orphan catcher shouted back.
Billie Jean reached the end of the tunnel –
"Ouch!"
And she burst through the wall of the cell.

"NO – NEVERRRRRRR
NO – woof."

Rover stopped singing when he saw the cops.
"Who are you?" said Kayla.

"Who are you?" said Not-Nice.

"Who are you?" said Billie Jean.

"Who are you?" said the orphan catcher.

"Who *are* you?" said Billie Jean.

"I'm the bank manager's sister," said the orphan catcher. "I mean, I'm the orphan catcher."

"Let go of my children," said Billie Jean.

"No," said the orphan catcher.

"I'm their mother, that's their father. That makes them not-orphans."

"I don't care," said the orphan catcher. "I found them first."

"Let go," said Billie Jean.

"No."

"Let go," said Mister Mack.

"No."

"Let go!" said Robbie and Jimmy.

"Uh-uh," said the orphan catcher.

Kayla jumped off Billie Jean's back and walked over to the orphan catcher. She got down on her little knees and she looked straight into the orphan catcher's eyes.

And she spoke.

"Who are you."

And she head-butted the orphan catcher.

Really?

No, she didn't. And Noodles just walked under a bus.

I forgot. Sorry!

Noodles walked into the cell.

"Are yis having a sing-song?" he said.

Good old Noodles. He loves a sing-song.

No one was singing, so Noodles walked back out.

Kayla looked straight into the orphan catcher's eyes.

"Who are you."

"That's better," said the orphan catcher.

She let go of the ankles and, slowly, slowly, her head dropped down. The tile clicked back into place.

Here is what Kayla actually said: "Let go, *please*."

The orphan catcher's mucky head popped back up again.

"Good manners cost nothing," she said, and the head dropped under the tile again. "Bye-bye."

And now, Billie Jean smiled at Mister Mack.

"What kept you?" said Mister Mack.

Billie Jean went to the door and slammed it.

"I missed you," she said.

She spoke to Nice and Not-Nice.

"Who are youse?"

"We're well-known detectives," said Not-Nice. "And you're under arrest."

He felt a sharp pain in his knee. It was Victoria, and she'd just bitten him.

"Batteries *not* included," she said.

"OK, OK," said Not-Nice. "You're

not under arrest."

"Thank you," said Billie Jean. "But why have you arrested my all-time favourite husband?"

"Well," said Nice. (Not-Nice was afraid to speak. There was a little girl staring at his knee.) "He tried to rob the bank."

"He didn't," said Billie Jean. "He was trying to get a loan."

"Really?" said Nice. "That's wonderful. But what about the gun?"

"Not a gun," said Billie Jean. "A saw."

"But it looks very like a gun."

"So what?" said Jimmy. "You look very like an eejit."

"I get your point," said Nice, who knew he looked like an eejit and wasn't a bit insulted. "But one last thing," he said.

He spoke to Billie Jean.

"What about you?"

"What about me?"

"Were you, by any chance, hiding away, waiting for Mister Mack here to join you with the loot?"

"No, I wasn't," said Billie Jean.

"Oh, good," said Nice. "But where were you?"

And Billie Jean smiled.

"My name is Billie Jean Fleetwood-Mack, and I just went around the world without telling anyone. And now I claim the record."

"Congratulations," said Nice.

"Batteries included," Victoria growled at Not-Nice's knee.

"Congratulations!" said Not-Nice.

CHAPTER TWENTY-FOUR

THE DAILY OUTRAGE

OUR HEROES COME HOME,

writes Our Special Correspondent,
Paddy Hackery.

There was dancing in the streets last night as superheroes Billie Jean Fleetwood-Mack and her husband, Mister, returned to their house in – ouch!

Paddy Hackery was bitten on the knee by a little girl.

And that, really, is the end of the story.

Mister Mack went back to inventing. He invented a clever device for helping prisoners escape from prison. (Hint: it looked very like a key.) And he was inventing a tunnel digger for Robbie and Jimmy when he got a phone call. It was Mister Kimberley, his old boss at the biscuit factory.

"It's good news, Mister Mack," said Mister Kimberley. "The people of Ireland aren't interested in keeping fit any more."

"Oh good," said Mister Mack.

"They're eating biscuits again."

"Oh great," said Mister Mack.

"So we're opening the factory again."

"Oh wonderful," said Mister Mack.

"Will you come back to us, Mister Mack?"

"I'm on my way," said Mister Mack. "Hang on, though. What about the cream crackers?"

"They're too healthy and useless," said Mister Kimberley. "No one wants them. They're gone."

"Yippee!" said Mister Mack.

He threw the phone into the air.

"We'll be back," said the cream cracker in Mister Mack's head, the one that always spoiled his daydreams. "Isn't that interesting?"

But Mister Mack wasn't listening. He was looking for his shoes. He was on his way to work. He could already taste the figs and chocolate.

"I'm a working man again!" he shouted as he ran to the door.

"You've always worked for me," said Billie Jean.

She kissed him as he ran past her, out the door.

Billie Jean was a working woman. She was a Dublin firefighter, fighting factory fires and forest fires and house fires, saving lots of people and trees.

"It's a bit boring," she said. "But I like the quiet life."

Billie Jean had broken all the records she'd ever wanted – the first woman to put out a forest fire without using water. So she started training Kayla. Youngest girl to swim the English Channel. Youngest girl to run across the Sahara. They even persuaded Mister Mack to come with them now and again. Youngest girl to climb Everest carrying her father on her back.

Robbie and Jimmy had enjoyed their tunnel digging and it became their hobby, after school. They tunnelled into shops and put men's clothes in the women's department and women's clothes in the men's department. They put fat men's underpants in the babies' department and nappies in the frozen food. They tunnelled into other tunnels, until Dublin was on top of one huge tunnel. A dog called Noodles started to sing –

"IT'S
SUCH A PER-FECT DAY-YYYY –"

And Dublin collapsed into the tunnel.

Victoria also became a record breaker. Her adventures had left her with a love of falling through the air, and that was what she did for the rest of her life. She also became a surgeon. And, once, she performed a heart transplant just seconds after herself and the patient jumped out of a plane. By the time they landed, the patient had a brand-new heart. He landed on a bed in the middle of a field, and the old heart landed in a swimming pool, in the middle of the hundred-metre freestyle.

The orphan catcher also had a

change of heart. She decided that orphan catching wasn't very nice, just after the Gigglers made her walk into the you-know-what. So, she started catching butterflies instead. But she wasn't very good at that either.

"I am not a butterfly, madam. I am a vegetarian rat."

Nice and Not-Nice changed too. They still worked as a team, but Nice became less nice, and Not-Nice became much nicer. Five months after they'd arrested Mister Mack, they became the exact same, for five minutes. They were known as the Twins, but only for ten minutes.

And the Gigglers got both of them. Just at the end of the ten minutes, the Not-Nice Twins were running down the street, chasing kids who'd done nothing except belch when they were walking past the Garda station. The kids turned a corner, and the Twins turned the corner and stepped on to twin poos, put there by the Gigglers

and delivered by Rover and his nephew, a mad young hound called Darren.

Rover retired. Kind of. As the kids got older, he became less interested in their adventures.

"Oh no! I've got spots on my chin. Rover, help!"

"Grow a beard, pal."

"I'm a girl."

"Walk around backwards till the spots go."

He could sort out most of their problems without standing up. But, now and again, a real adventure came his way.

"Oh no, there's a meteorite heading towards Earth. That means I'll only be able to wear my new trainers once before we die."

"How long have we got till the meteorite hits?"

"Two hours."

"No sweat."

He still sold his poo to the Gigglers – they couldn't depend on young Darren – and he became even richer. He was the first dog to own a football club when he bought Manchester United. And Manchester United became the first club to win the F.A. Cup with a poodle in goal. The poodle was female, and her name was Amanda.

Klaus kept losing shoes. But then he lost a leg as well, and all his troubles were over. He recorded a CD of Irish songs, and a duet with Sinéad O'Connor: "One Love, Two Voices, Three Legs." The slugs never tried to take over the world again, but they did take over a cabbage in a field near the Macks' house. And what about the budgies? They opened a new pet shop and they made a fortune selling the people who came into the shop to the rabbits who were already in the shop. All over Dublin, people went about their daily lives, but only because their pet rabbits let them.

"A rabbit is a burrowing animal with long ears and a fluffy tail. Isn't that interesting?"

OH NO! THE MESSAGES!

All good stories have messages, and this story has none. But here are a few anyway.

1. If you work in a bank and a man walks in with something that looks like a machine gun, it might really be a machine gun. If he says, "Give me all the cash," it probably *is* a machine gun. If, however, he says, "I'm here to fix the shelves," it is probably a saw.

2. If you ever meet a dog called Noodles, get him to sing "Bohemian Rhapsody". He'll do it for nothing, and he's brilliant.

3. The next time your father's in jail, make sure he gives you the car keys before he's locked up.

4. If you are a nice detective, you shouldn't smoke. It's bad for you, and prisoners will escape, using the matches that you drop on the floor.

5. If you ever perform a heart

transplant in mid-air, make sure you bring a flask, because you'll probably want a cup of coffee about halfway through the operation.

6. The next time you're feeding your rabbit, look into his or her big eyes and ask yourself: "Is this my rabbit, or am I this rabbit's human?"

7. If you are allergic to Irish music, stay well away from Germany. France and South Africa are safe, but be careful in Sweden, and Irish music of the most vicious kind has been known to hide in the bushes and pubs of Boston.

8. If an orphan catcher is grabbing your ankle, if a lion is about to bite your bum, if an angry bus is about to run over your head, always remember to say, "Please." It's a magic little word and it might just save your life.

THE END

Hey, pal.

There's a little word missing, Rover.

Hey, pal, *please*.

Oh, yes. Sorry, Rover. I nearly forgot.

9. If you're a poodle and your name is Amanda, Rover says, "Keep your football boots polished, Baby. Your big day is coming."

THE END